Joseph was in the library, waiting for his dad. He was kneeling on the floor by the Oversize Books Section, reading *An Illustrated History of Football*. Then he heard the beep of a car horn.

"That's your dad," said Helen, who was in his class at school. "He sounds in a hurry."

"He always is," said Joseph. "Sometimes I wish you could change dads, the way you can change library books. I wish there was a Dad Library."

"Oh, but there is," said Helen.

Joseph is fed up with his dad. He forgets to go shopping; he cooks terrible meals, he doesn't help Joseph with his homework and he makes him eat school dinners. Then Joseph discovers the Dad Library, crammed full with all sorts of wonderful dads. Should he borrow an Organizer Dad, or a Sporting Dad, or a Clever Dad, or an Indulgent Dad? Joseph wants to try them all. But which one will he want to keep?

www.kidsatrandomhouse.co.uk

the Dad Library

DENNIS WHELEHAN
ILLUSTRATED BY TIM ARCHBOLD

YOUNG CORGI BOOKS

For Timothy and Ben

THE DAD LIBRARY
A YOUNG CORGI BOOK : 0 552 529796

First publication in Great Britain

PRINTING HISTORY
Young Corgi edition published 1997

5 7 9 10 8 6 4

Text copyright © 1997 by Dennis Whelehan
Illustrations copyright © 1997 by Tim Archbold

The right of Dennis Whelehan to be identified as the author of this
work has been asserted in accordance with the Copyright, Designs and
Patents Act 1988

Condition of Sale
This book is sold subject to the condition that it shall not, by way of
trade or otherwise, be lent, re-sold, hired out or otherwise circulated
without the publisher's prior consent in any form of binding or cover
other than that in which it is published and without a similar condition
including this condition being imposed on the subsequent purchaser.

Set in 17/23pt Bembo Schoolbook by Phoenix Typesetting,
Ilkley, West Yorkshire.

Young Corgi Books are published by Random House Children's Books,
61–63 Uxbridge Road, London W5 5SA,
a division of The Random House Group Ltd,
in Australia by Random House Australia (Pty) Ltd,
20 Alfred Street, Milsons Point, Sydney, NSW 2061, Australia,
and in New Zealand by Random House New Zealand Ltd,
18 Poland Road, Glenfield, Auckland 10, New Zealand
and in South Africa by Random House (Pty) Ltd,
Endulini, 5a Jubilee Road, Parktown 2193, South Africa.

Printed and bound in Great Britain by
Cox & Wyman Ltd, Reading, Berkshire

CONTENTS

CONTENTS

CHAPTER ONE

Joseph was in the library,
waiting for his dad. He was
kneeling on the floor by the
Oversize Books Section, reading
An Illustrated History of Football.

Then he heard the beep of a car horn.

"That's your dad," said Helen, who was in his class at school. "He sounds in a hurry."

"He always is," said Joseph. "Sometimes I wish you could change dads, the way you can change library books. I wish there was a Dad Library."

"Oh, but there is," said Helen.

But already Joseph's dad was standing before them, in shirt

sleeves, with his tie undone and a worried look on his face.

"We're late," he said, and shoved *An Illustrated History of Football* back on the shelf.

Next he grabbed Joseph by the arm and propelled him through the exit. Joseph knew his dad didn't mean to be rough, but he

still had to jump down the library steps to keep up.

Helen was watching through a window.

"Tell me tomorrow," Joseph yelled.

His dad bundled him into the car.

"Fingers, seat belt," he said, and slammed the door.

Joseph's dad tried to make conversation as they drove to the hospital, to show they were good friends. They were visiting Joseph's mum, who was recovering from an operation for appendicitis.

"Anything interesting happen in school?"

"Not really. That football book was great. I wouldn't mind having it."

"Keep up the good work," said his dad.

Joseph sighed. Mum always said his dad never listened. "Talk to the cat," was what she said.

"I'd like a mountain bike too," said Joseph, half to himself. How nice it would be to have a dad who would buy you anything you wanted. An Indulgent Dad.

"What's for supper?" Joseph asked.

His dad took one hand off the steering wheel and hit himself on the forehead.

"I forgot to do the shopping," he said.

"We'll look in the fridge," said Joseph. It was what they usually did.

But wouldn't it be convenient to

have a dad who remembered to
do the shopping and could cook
decent meals? Were there any
Organizer Dads on the shelves of
the Dad Library?

Visiting had already started when
they reached the hospital. Joseph's
mum was sitting up in bed. She
wore more make-up than usual,
and a new tortoiseshell comb in
her hair.

"I hope you have been eating properly," was the first thing she said when they were seated at the bedside.

"No problem," said Joseph's dad.

"Marvellous meals," said Joseph, who wasn't one to tell tales.

His mum glanced from one to the other.

"I've got a pair of fibbers," she said, smiling. "Like father, like son."

Later in the evening, after a supper of beans on toast, Joseph got on with his homework: a project on famous explorers.

He went to his dad for help.

"Who was Captain Scott?"

His dad was reading the paper, and kept his eyes on the page as he answered.

"He went to the South Pole. Or was it the North Pole?"

Imagine having a dad who could help you with your homework, whatever the subject. A Clever Dad.

That night Joseph had a nightmare. It wasn't very scary, but he called out just the same. His dad staggered into his bedroom, dazed after being woken up.

"Take it easy," he said, and sat

on the side of the bed. "What
was it this time?"

"Tigers," said Joseph.

"Cheer up, next time it might
be kittens."

"Or lambs," said Joseph.

"Or day-old chicks."

Joseph laughed. His dad sat
with his arm around him until
eventually he went back to sleep.

The next morning at breakfast,
Joseph had a row with his dad.

"What's in my sandwiches?" he
asked.

"You'll have to stay to school
dinner," said his dad.

Joseph clutched his throat,
crossed his eyes and stuck out his
tongue.

"It's only for today."

"That's what you said yesterday. And the day before."

It was pelting with rain when they were ready to leave.

"I'll get my wellingtons," said Joseph.

He went to the cupboard under the stairs and gave the door two bangs with his fist. It sprang open.

"Look at your hair," said his dad. He unhooked a clothes brush from behind the cupboard door and pretended to brush Joseph's hair. It was a family joke.

"What about a lift?" Joseph

shouted as they ran through the
rain to the car.

"Sorry, I'm late, you'll have to
walk."

"But I'll get soaked."

"See you in the library. Take care."

The first person Joseph met as he struggled out of his dripping anorak in the school cloakroom was Helen. He felt just in the mood to get his own back on his dad.

First there was the forgotten shopping and the awful meals, then the failure to help with homework, then the school dinners, and finally this trek through a downpour.

"Where's the Dad Library?"

"I'll show you after school," said Helen.

That afternoon Joseph walked with Helen to the rear of the public library, where there was a garden with seats and flowerbeds.

Parked in the garden was a long
caravan made of shiny metal. It
had round windows, like
portholes in a ship, and wooden
steps leading up to an open door.

"That's it?" said Joseph.

"That's the Dad Library," said
Helen, and waved him goodbye.

CHAPTER TWO

Joseph climbed the steps and
entered the library.

"Name and address." The
librarian behind the desk wore a
straw hat, decorated with fruit.
Pink, heart-shaped glasses hung
from a chain around her neck.

"How many dads can I take
out at a time?" asked Joseph.

The librarian ducked her head,
then raised it suddenly, like a
startled deer. The glasses landed
securely on her nose.

"Only one. And the fines are astronomical. A whole year's pocket money for just one day overdue."

She tapped briskly on a computer keyboard, then handed Joseph a card in a green plastic wallet.

Joseph thanked her and went into the library. It was full of dads! He walked past rows of them, standing perfectly still on shelves raised a few feet above the ground.

He read the cards above their heads: Gardening Dads – Sporting Dads – Organizer Dads

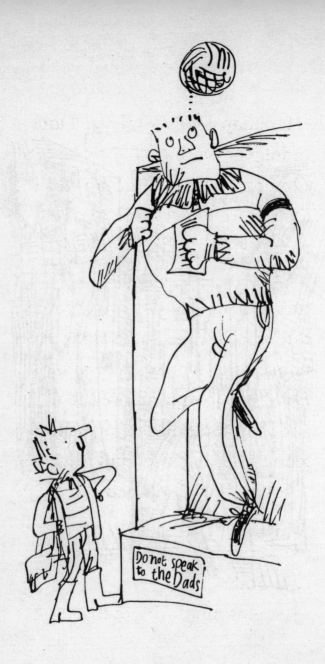

Do not speak
to the Dads

– Holiday Dads – Clever Dads –
Indulgent Dads.

Joseph examined a Sporting
Dad more closely. He was
wearing an orange tracksuit.
Instead of standing still, he was
running on the spot and heading
a football at the same time. A
notice said, *Do not speak to the
Dads*, but Joseph ignored it.

"I play football for my school
team," he said cheerfully.

"Train hard," gasped the
Sporting Dad. "Up at dawn, run
twenty miles a day, take lots of
cold baths."

Joseph thought he didn't look

like someone who'd enjoy a kick-
about in the park, so he moved
on to the Organizer Dads. There
was a wide choice: dads in
overalls, dads in uniforms, dads in
suits, dads with paint brushes and
hammers, dads with briefcases
and mobile phones.

Joseph finally decided on one
with lots of useful things sticking
out of his pockets, such as
coloured pencils, lengths of string,
batteries and rolls of Sellotape.
He took the Organizer Dad to
the desk. The librarian repeated
her trick with the heart-shaped
glasses, and stamped the issue

label pinned to his chest.

Just then Joseph's real dad came
bounding into the library.

"We're late," he said. But
before he could grab Joseph, the

librarian placed him on a trolley
with the other dads who had
been returned and were waiting
to be put back on the shelves.

As they left the library, the
Organizer Dad handed Joseph a
walkie-talkie.
  "Good communication is the
secret of successful organization,"
he said.

"Could we do some shopping?"
Joseph asked.

The Organizer Dad unrolled a
shopping list that was at least a
foot long.

"Let's go," he said.

Once inside the supermarket,
the Organizer Dad left Joseph in
charge of the trolley while he

sprinted off down the aisle.

Joseph waited. The walkie-talkie crackled.

"Prepare to receive shopping."

Tins of beans, jars of jam and

boxes of teabags flew over the shelf units for Joseph to catch and load into the trolley. Sometimes

he missed. A jar of honey burst
with a loud plop, but he
managed to save a bottle of
pickled gherkins by diving full
length. He tossed it up in the air
again, pretending to be a
cricketer on television.

The walkie-talkie crackled once
more.

"Prepare for mobile shopping."

Next moment Joseph was
kneeling in the trolley. The
Organizer Dad pushed frantically
from behind. They swept through
the aisles of the supermarket like
a bobsleigh, zig-zagging to avoid
startled customers. Joseph was

beginning to enjoy himself.
Shopping had never been such
fun.

"Washing powder," shouted the
Organizer Dad. Joseph leant out
and snatched a packet from a tall
stack. The stack wobbled, then
collapsed slowly like a dynamited
tower block.

At the checkout, the Organizer Dad paid with the exact money. He had recorded all the purchases on a calculator.

That evening the Organizer Dad worked out the sandwich fillings for Joseph's packed lunches for the next two years. He also prepared a meal that smelled delicious and tasted even better.

"What's in it?" asked Joseph, eating ravenously.

"Steak, ice-cream, jelly, mushrooms, chocolate, strawberries, roast potatoes."

"I didn't know you could mix

all those together," said Joseph,
swallowing the last mouthful.

"You can if you're organized,"
said the Organizer Dad.

The next morning before
breakfast the Organizer Dad
tidied all the drawers and
cupboards in the house. He
couldn't open the cupboard under

the stairs where Joseph kept his wellingtons.

"It's easy," said Joseph, and gave the door two hard bangs with his fist. The door jumped open.

"That won't do," said the Organizer Dad. "I'll have to fix that."

He hurried off to get his tools.

Joseph didn't want the door fixed. Opening it was a trick he did when friends came to visit.

Besides, it had always been like that, as long as he could remember. He tried to argue, but the Organizer Dad wouldn't listen.

"It looks disorganized," he said. "We can't have that."

When Joseph came home from school, the cupboard door opened normally, without any bangs, like any boring old door anywhere.

The nice thing about the Dad Library was that you didn't have to put up with a dad once you got tired of him. Joseph returned the Organizer Dad to the library that very evening after school.

He had a quick look at the shelf

labelled *Ordinary Dads*, expecting
to see his real dad standing there.
The shelf was empty.

"Probably in the stockroom," said Joseph to himself. After all, what demand could there be for Ordinary Dads, when there were lots of better dads just standing on the shelves waiting to be stamped and taken out?

CHAPTER THREE

The next dad Joseph borrowed
was a Clever Dad.

"Will you help me with my
homework?" Joseph asked as they
walked home. "I've got to do a
project on explorers. Do you
know anything about Captain
Scott?"

The Clever Dad closed the encyclopaedia he had been reading.

"I know everything about Captain Scott," he replied. "In fact, I am the world authority.

I am very highly qualified, with degrees in lots of subjects, including History, Mathematics, Philosophy, Mechanical Engineering and seventeen foreign languages. I'm not just clever, I'm a genius."

Joseph thought he was very boastful and long-winded. He had staring eyes and fluffy white hair, like a mad inventor in a comic.

Joseph was wondering if they were too far from the library to go back and return him when they paused to cross the road. A van had stalled at the traffic

lights, and a long queue of cars
sounded their horns impatiently.
Joseph remembered that the
Clever Dad had mentioned
mechanical engineering.

"Can you get that car started?"
Joseph asked.

"My knowledge is purely
theoretical," said the Clever Dad,
sounding very superior.

Joseph wasn't sure what that meant, but he found out when he got the Clever Dad home. He brought some broken toys into the kitchen. A Clever Dad ought to be able to mend broken toys.

"Think you could fix my steam-engine?"

"Ah," said the Clever Dad, "steam was so important in the development of our industries. And the railways—"

"What about this plane?" Joseph interrupted.

He handed the Clever Dad his flying model Spitfire.

"We have the Wright brothers to thank for powered flight," said the Clever Dad in a monotonous voice. "Of course, the invention of the jet engine—"

"This will only turn very slowly," said Joseph, holding a wind-up Merry-Go-Round he got

for Christmas when he was little.
"It's just a Misery-Go-Round."

He knew it was a weak joke.
The Clever Dad ignored him
completely.

"Also known as a 'carousel',
and popular in fairgrounds
throughout the world—"

Joseph ran and switched on the
television to escape the boring
lectures spouting out of the
Clever Dad. Luckily it was one of

his favourite programmes, a quiz-show called *Sharpen Your Wits*.

The Clever Dad answered the first question, which was about Roman history, before the quizmaster had finished asking it.

"Good guess," said Joseph,

which was what he said to his real dad whenever he got anything right.

"Guess!" said the Clever Dad. "A genius like me never guesses."

He was still muttering indignantly when they finally reached a question that Joseph could do.

"Name the England side that won the World Cup in 1966."

Joseph began: "Banks, Cohen, Wilson, Stiles, Charlton J.—"

"Moore, Ball, Hurst, Hunt, Charlton R., Peters," interrupted the Clever Dad. "And what's more, I know the names of all the teams participating in the competition."

"I bet you didn't see the Final at Wembley," Joseph said.

"Neither did you," said the Clever Dad.

"My real dad saw it," said Joseph. "He gave me his ticket."

"Well, I've seen all the games on video," said the Clever Dad.

Joseph felt totally fed up. Really, it was like being in the school playground, only worse.

The Clever Dad kept his promise, however, and helped Joseph with his project.

"Write down everything that I dictate," said the Clever Dad, and began pacing back and forth and ruffling his fluffy white hair.

"Captain Scott's unsuccessful attempt to reach the South Pole was one of the most exciting events in Polar exploration."

The Clever Dad then gave list after list of facts, such as the weight of the anchor on Scott's

ship, the *Terra Nova*, the amount of food eaten each day, and the exact height of each member of the expedition. Joseph scribbled until his hand ached.

"This is turning into the most boring event in Polar exploration," said Joseph, and yawned a wide yawn. The Clever Dad continued pacing and dictating. Joseph's head sank slowly on to his pile of notes, and with the Clever Dad's voice echoing distantly in his ears, he fell asleep.

By the next morning, Joseph had almost decided to return the Clever Dad to the Dad Library. He was boastful, he was boring, he used long words – but he certainly was clever. Then something happened that helped Joseph to make up his mind.

Just before he left for school,

Joseph handed the Clever Dad
the clothes brush from the
cupboard beneath the stairs.

The Clever Dad brushed his
own jacket, then hung the brush
on its hook.

"You're supposed to pretend to
brush my hair," said Joseph.

For the very first time, the Clever Dad looked puzzled.

"It's a family joke," Joseph explained.

"Absolutely preposterous," said the Clever Dad.

That did it. Joseph returned the Clever Dad on his way to school. He had another quick look on the shelves for his real dad. There was still no sign of him.

Joseph was about to say, "They've decided to leave him in the stockroom," when he had a worrying thought. Suppose his real dad had actually been borrowed? Suppose he couldn't

get him back whenever he
wanted to?

"I'll cross that bridge when I
come to it," said Joseph,
repeating a favourite saying of
his mum's.

Meanwhile, he knew which dad
he wanted next. He would collect
him immediately after school.

CHAPTER FOUR

The third dad that Joseph
borrowed was the only one of
that category left on the shelf.
  "You're lucky to find him," said
the librarian, who was now
wearing a black hat with a wide
brim pinned up on one side, like
a soldier in the U.S. cavalry.

"These Indulgent Dads are the second most popular dads we've got."

She attached a new label to the Indulgent Dad's chest, because the old one was used up, and stamped the date for return.

Joseph didn't like to ask who the most popular dads were, in case it hurt the Indulgent Dad's feelings.

"You don't look much different from my real dad," Joseph said when they got outside. He was wearing an old sweater like the one his real dad wore at

weekends, the one with holes in the elbows.

"I smile a lot more," said the Indulgent Dad, "and no matter what you do, I never shout. I give you anything you ask for, and let you do whatever you like. That's what *indulgent* means."

On the way home they passed a bike shop. Joseph thought it would be a good chance to try the Indulgent Dad out.

"I'd like that mountain bike," said Joseph, pointing to the most expensive model in the window.

"Of course," said the Indulgent Dad.

In addition to the mountain
bike, they bought a streamlined
crash helmet, a Tour de France
cycling jersey and a set of
panniers.

There was a sweet shop next
door.

"I fancy some sweets," said
Joseph, pushing his luck.

"What a good idea," said the
Indulgent Dad.

They bought four boxes of
chocolates, two bags of assorted
toffees, and a whole jar of
liquorice bootlaces.

"Sure that's enough?" asked the
Indulgent Dad.

"Enough for the moment,
thanks," said Joseph politely.

That evening Joseph was allowed to ride his mountain bike down the stairs, out the kitchen door, across the flowerbeds in the garden, in the front door and round and round the living room. He did that until he was exhausted, eighty-three circuits in all.

"What time is bedtime?" Joseph asked.

He had seen the football on television, and was watching a film that went on until after midnight.

"Whenever you like," said the Indulgent Dad.

Joseph stayed up until three o'clock in the morning. He got

into bed fully dressed, including
his shoes.

Shortly after dropping off to
sleep, Joseph had a nightmare. It
was a particularly bad one,
brought on by chocolates, toffees
and liquorice bootlaces.

"Dad!" he shouted.

He could hear
snoring from along
the landing.

"Dad!"

He got out of bed and knocked
on the Indulgent Dad's bedroom
door. The snoring continued. He
turned the door knob, crossed the
room, and shook the Indulgent
Dad by the shoulder.

"I had a nightmare," he said.

The Indulgent Dad peered at the illuminated dial of the alarm clock by his bed.

"Please go back to bed," mumbled the Indulgent Dad.

"Will you come and sit with me?" Joseph asked.

"I'm afraid I can't," said the Indulgent Dad in a weak voice.

"I don't usually stay up late. Looking after you has worn me out."

The Indulgent Dad pulled the duvet up to his ears. Within seconds he was snoring again.

Joseph returned to his bedroom. He put the light on, sat on his bed, and had a big think.

So far he had borrowed an Organizer Dad, a Clever Dad and an Indulgent Dad. Nobody could say they weren't useful, because they were. They even made a fuss of you, like uncles or family friends. But they weren't fun all the time,

and sometimes they could be
pretty clueless.

Joseph sighed. The truth was
that he missed his real dad, who
knew the importance of things
like cupboard doors, family jokes
and nightmares.

The following morning at
breakfast, Joseph's mum

telephoned from the hospital.

"Dad isn't here at the moment,"
Joseph said truthfully, when she
asked to speak to him.

"When are you two coming to
see me?"

Joseph made his mind up very
quickly.

"We are coming to see you tonight."

As soon as he had returned the Indulgent Dad, Joseph ran to the shelf marked *Ordinary Dads*. It was empty. He went in search of the librarian.

"I'd like to take my real dad out, please."

The librarian, who was wearing a police motor-cyclist's helmet, raised the visor to consult her computer screen.

"He's due back today," she said.

"That's a bit of luck," said
Joseph.

"But he's already been reserved
for the next eighteen months."

"Oh, no!" said Joseph.

"He's an Ordinary Dad, and

we've only got one of those,"
explained the librarian. "Didn't
you realize that he's the most
popular dad in the library?"

CHAPTER FIVE

Joseph filled in a reserve form and
asked the librarian what time
they closed.

"We never close. Open twenty-four hours a day, including Christmas."

Suppose his dad wasn't returned by the end of visiting hours at the hospital? He would have to tell his mum about the Dad Library, and he'd rather not. And even if he was returned, there was that

matter of an eighteen month wait.

An hour passed, then another. Dads were being returned all the time, but not the one he wanted. It was hot, and very quiet. Joseph felt tired after his broken sleep the previous night. He yawned, and closed his eyes.

He opened them with a start. It was already dark outside. A girl with red hair was arguing loudly with the librarian.

"You can't renew the date on that dad," said the librarian patiently, "because he's already reserved, over and over again."

"I don't care," shrieked the girl. She collapsed on the floor and started to sob.

"He's the best dad in the whole world."

Joseph craned his neck to see
who they were arguing about.

Who else could it be but his real
dad? And that's exactly who it
was.

While the librarian was busy
explaining the borrowing rules,
Joseph tiptoed up to his dad and
took him by the hand.

"Make a run for it," he
whispered.

"How can we?" said his dad.

The red-haired girl was sobbing
more loudly than ever. The
librarian, who was kneeling on

the floor trying to comfort her,
was blocking the only exit.

Then Joseph remembered the
portholes that served as windows
in the walls of the library.

"Quick, back this way."

Together Joseph and his dad
hurried into the library. The
portholes were fastened with

metal clamps, just as on a ship.

"They're too stiff," said Joseph's dad, pushing and tugging. "We'll never escape now."

"Yes we will," said Joseph.

He began searching the shelves for a Sporting Dad. At last he found the one he wanted – a weightlifter.

"Can you open one of the portholes, please?" Joseph asked.

"Glad to be of service," said the
Sporting Dad, and flexed his
muscular arm.

He opened the porthole without
any trouble.

Joseph remembered to return
him to his shelf before helping his
dad to squeeze through the
narrow opening. It was much
easier for Joseph.

They held hands and didn't stop
running until they were safely
clear of the library gardens.

Immediately they arrived home,

Joseph unpinned the issue label
from his dad's chest.

"You won't be needing that
again," he said.

Later that evening they visited
Joseph's mum in hospital. She
was completely recovered,

waiting with her suitcase packed,
all ready to come home.

"How tidy the drawers are," she
said when she saw the kitchen.

"And what a huge stock of food
you've got."

Joseph hung her coat in the cupboard under the stairs, and the door opened without any bangs.

"Someone's been busy," she said to his dad, who exchanged raised eyebrows with Joseph and gave a modest smile.

Joseph offered his mum a chocolate he found in the bottom of a box, and told her about the two house points he got for his project on Captain Scott. Then he posed on his mountain bike, so that she could take a flash-photo for the family album. There were some suspicious-looking tyre marks on the living-room carpet,

but she made no comment.

He stayed up later than usual because his mum said it was a special occasion. When he finally went to bed his dad came and sat beside him.

"Did you hate it in the Dad Library?" Joseph asked.

"It got a bit lonely. I didn't much like the children who took me out."

"I didn't much like the dads I borrowed," Joseph admitted.

Then he had an idea, and

decided to ask his dad for his opinion.

"Do you think," he said, "that there is a Child Library, just like the Dad Library?"

His dad shrugged, and leant across to switch off the bedside lamp.

"It's a possibility. If there were, I'd choose you."

"What sort of children would there be on the shelves? I bet there'd be a Tidy Child, and an Obedient Child, and probably a Polite Child—"

"Go to sleep," interrupted his dad. "You've got school tomorrow."

Joseph punched a hollow in his pillow, and settled down to sleep.

"Would you always choose me?" he asked.

"Always," said his dad. "I'd keep you out and pretend you were lost."

"Astronomical fines," said Joseph drowsily.

But his dad had already closed the bedroom door, and didn't hear.

THE END

GO FOX
by Helen Dunmore

'Keep going, Go Fox!
You've got to make it!
Go, go, go, Go Fox!'

Danny loves his new computer game, Go Fox.
With Danny's help, clever little Go Fox can
escape the dreaded Spook Tree, swim the raging
river – and try and dodge the greedy green
snappers!

Then suddenly Go Fox pops out of the
computer screen, and Danny's in big trouble. Go
Fox is hungry, and bubble-gum and beans on
toast just won't do. What he wants is melt-in-
the-mouth chicken and tender little rabbits!

Can Danny keep his new friend happy, and
keep him a secret too – or will the adventure of
the chase tempt Go Fox back into the game?

Published by Young Corgi Books, available
from all good book stores.

0 552 52963 X

YOUNG CORGI BOOKS